Giving the Best of What You Have

Sulaiman Learns the Blessings of Giving

Aliya Vaughan

THE ISLAMIC
FOUNDATION

Giving the Best of What You Have –
Sulaiman Learns the Blessings of Giving

First Published in 2025 by
THE ISLAMIC FOUNDATION

Distributed by
KUBE PUBLISHING LTD
Tel +44 (0)1530 249230, Fax +44 (0)1530 249656
E-mail: info@kubepublishing.com
Website: www.kubepublishing.com

Author Aliya Vaughan
Illustrator Anisa Mohammed
(Art style based on illustrations by Rakaiya Azzouz)
Book design Nasir Cadir

A Cataloguing-in-Publication Data record for this book is available from the British Library

ISBN 978-1-83592-014-5
eISBN 978-1-83592-015-2

Printed by IMAK, Turkey

Contents

‘By no means shall you attain righteousness unless you give (freely) of that which you love. And whatever you spend; indeed, Allah is Knowing of it.’

Surah Al ‘Imran (3:92)

Indeed! Charity is the best investment in this life for the next.

Acknowledgements

I would like to offer my sincere thanks to the team at Kube for all their work on this series; to Rakaiya Azzouz for beautifully illustrating the four previous books and to Anisa Mohammed for illustrating the fifth book in the Sulaiman series. I would also like to thank lawyer, Saniya Hussain for freely and patiently sharing her knowledge on the UK asylum and refugee legal process.

The Prophet, (ﷺ), said,

"Whoever does not thank people has not thanked Allah."

Narrated by Abu Hurairah; at-Tirmidhi, Sunan Abi Dawud, al-Adab al-Mufrad

Chapter 1

The distinct rustle of sweet wrappers could be heard above the noise of the vacuum cleaner. Sulaiman thought his mum's cleaning would drown it out, but Musa had bat-like precision hearing.

"I want some!" Musa whined chasing Sulaiman along the passage as he quickly disappeared into the bathroom. "Gimme some!" Musa wailed, banging on the locked door with his little fists. Hannah was in the next room trying on her Eid outfit.

"Where did he get those sweets from?" she muttered curiously, trying to look through the crack in the bathroom door, but it had been blocked with a towel.

"Sulaiman! Remember what Mum said; those sweets are for tomorrow… and you know you're not supposed to eat in the bathroom!" she bellowed. Now there were two pairs of fists pummelling on the door. After several moments the door creaked opened. Musa tried to push his way in, but Sulaiman had blocked the door with his foot.

"It's too late, they've all gone!" he teased, opening his mouth wide to reveal his bright crimson jelly-stained tongue. "It was a tiny packet anyway."

"It doesn't matter," Hannah retorted, her face flushing red in annoyance. "You should have shared them. There're blessings in sharing."

Sulaiman opened the door wide and dropped the empty sweet packet just above Musa's head. It cascaded gracefully in the air and landed at Musa's feet. Musa let out a piercing shriek and ran to his mum to snitch on his brother.

"That's selfish," Hannah protested. "I always share with you." It was true. Out of the three of them, Hannah was the most generous and would always give freely, but Sulaiman wasn't so open-handed.

"It's not that deep. I'll give you some of mine tomorrow... if you're good to me." He smirked, flicking Hannah's nose as he brushed past her.

"Too late and you're not doing me a favour." She growled disgruntled, storming back to her room. "You had your chance and you blew it, and now you're going to be in trouble with mum."

"Whatever!" Sulaiman shrugged waving his hand dismissively.

Chapter 2

The next day after the Eid prayer, Sulaiman was keen to try out his new gift: a remote-control car. His dad agreed he could play with it in the lane next to their flat. Gently lifting the vehicle out of the box, he plugged in the battery and switched on the car. Holding the toy in one hand and pressing the controller with the other he watched the wheels spin and whirr loudly in midair.

"Alhamdulillah, they don't jam like my last one!" He smiled, placing it on the ground and pressing the controller again. Plumes of dust churned into the air as it hurtled up the gravel track with speed. After racing the car several laps up and down the lane, it hit a dip in the road causing it to spin out of control and smash into the fence. He ran to pick it up to inspect the damage.

"I had a car like that," an unfamiliar voice announced behind him.

Sulaiman turned in surprise, as he hadn't noticed anyone approaching. A boy holding a backpack was grinning, revealing the thick metal braces on his upper teeth. He had an accent, but Sulaiman couldn't detect where he was from.

"I could do tricks with it too," the boy declared confidently.

Sulaiman acknowledged him shyly trying not to stare at his jacket and trousers. He didn't look bad; just different to the other boys in the area. There was no damage to the car, so Sulaiman placed it back down onto the ground.

"I can show you if you like?" The boy insisted.

Can I trust him, though Sulaiman wondered hesitating, fearing the boy might run off with it, but he was eager to see what kind of tricks he could do.

"Okay, show me," Sulaiman agreed, handing the boy the controller. The boy beamed and threw his backpack to one side. He sprinted to the end of the track to make a ramp using a plank of wood and some broken bricks that were lying in some rubble. He ran back next to Sulaiman, re-positioned the car and pressed the controller. The car propelled up the track with speed towards the ramp. It accelerated high into the air, spun 360 degrees, and landed back down on its wheels again.

"Wow! how did you do that?" Sulaiman cried, holding his head with both hands in astonishment.

"Easy," the boy laughed, "you build the ramp up really high and make the car go really fast with lots of throttle!"

Sulaiman grabbed the controller and re-positioned the car. As the car gained speed, it mounted the ramp but lost control halfway up and fell off the side. Sulaiman frantically steered the wheel on the controller, but it was too late. The car had disappeared out of sight.

"Go get it then," the boy demanded impatiently.

"I can't," Sulaiman replied. "It's gone

behind the garages, and I'm not allowed to go there on my own."

"How are you going to get it back then?" asked the boy.

"It's okay, my dad's coming in a minute. I'll get it when he comes." The boys sat on the grass verge and chatted as they waited.

"I'm Sulaiman, by the way."

"I'm Joseph," the boy replied reaching out to offer him a fist bump. Sulaiman was surprised to learn that they were both the same age despite Joseph being much taller and broader. His laugh was warm and infectious. Not only did they share the same sense of humour, but they also liked similar sports and hobbies. After several minutes Sulaiman's dad and Musa came into view with another man accompanying them.

"I've got to go now," Joseph sighed. "That's my dad."

"Don't go yet," Sulaiman urged, "ask if you can play with my car for a bit longer."

Joseph glanced at his dad with pleading eyes. His father smiled and nodded.

"You'll be seeing a lot more of each other from now on," Sulaiman's dad remarked. "Joseph and his family have just moved to the area, and he'll be going to the same school as you."

"Race you to it then!" Sulaiman shouted and sprinted towards the garages to get the car. Joseph laughed loudly as he ran to catch up with him.

He can even run as fast as me! Sulaiman was glad, he liked a challenge.

Chapter 3

Sulaiman arrived early at school on Monday morning. He was chatting with his friends on the playground wall and sharing stories about their activities over the weekend.

"Who's that?" One of the boys asked pointing to a new boy walking through the school gates.

"Joseph!" Sulaiman shouted, springing

off the wall and dashing over to greet him. The anxiety on Joseph's face quickly melted away. He was relieved to see a friendly face. Sulaiman pulled Joseph by his jumper and introduced him to the rest of the boys one by one.

Most of them were welcoming, although one or two were not so friendly. Joseph noticed one boy was mocking the hole in his shoe making him feel awkward and uncomfortable. Sulaiman pretended not to notice. Suddenly the bell trilled loudly marking the beginning of a new school day. The children gathered up their belongings and lined up in straight, neat rows.

"Where do I go?" Joseph panicked.

"Stand with me," Sulaiman replied confidently. "I don't think it matters which line you're in, as you're new to the school aren't you?"

Joseph smiled and quickly shuffled up next to him. As they waited in line, Sulaiman playfully tugged on Joseph's backpack. Sniggering, Joseph yanked it back hard. All of a sudden, the tatty strap ripped away from the seam, causing all his books and pencils to spill onto the floor.

They laughed spontaneously as they watched bits of paper flying about in the wind. The commotion quickly attracted the attention of a teacher. She rushed forward clapping her hands in annoyance and gestured sternly for them to pick up the mess. Joseph scooped up the books and pencils and held them close to his chest, while Sulaiman gathered up the rest of the belongings that had gone astray.

"Inside you two," the teacher instructed. "Go to the secretary's office. She can give you another bag."

"Mrs. Peters is a bit strict," Sulaiman smirked.

The teacher clapped her hands again and pointed towards the door to indicate where they needed to go.

"What did you do over the weekend?" Sulaiman enquired casually as they entered the building.

"Not much," Joseph answered with a shrug. Sulaiman smiled and told Joseph about all his weekend activities instead.

Chapter 4

As the weeks passed Sulaiman and Joseph became firm friends. They did everything together. They sat next to each other in lessons, ate together in the canteen and played football in the playground during the break. Sulaiman also invited Joseph to his house a few times after school and at weekends. He trusted Joseph so much that he even lent him some of his games.

Although Sulaiman valued Joseph's friendship, he was concerned it was becoming a bit one-sided, so he decided to bring the subject up during a lunch break.

"We've been friends for a while now, but I've never been to your house. Why don't I come this weekend?" Sulaiman suggested.

"Er... we're a little busy this weekend. Perhaps another time," Joseph stammered awkwardly.

"You always say you're busy, but you also say your weekends are boring and that you never do anything," Sulaiman remarked.

"Are you calling me a liar?" Joseph snarled defensively.

"No. I just thought it'd be nice to go to your house for a change, instead of always coming to mine."

"If it's a problem I just won't come to your

house anymore," Joseph snapped angrily.

"I never said it was a problem... and I never said I didn't want you to come to my house. I just haven't seen where you live." Sulaiman hated arguing, so to keep the peace he backed down.

"Forget it," he sighed wearily. "We've got a maths lesson to go to."

* * *

That evening as Sulaiman ate dinner with his family, his mum noticed he was a bit quiet.

"Is something bothering you, Sulaiman?" she asked concerned.

He shook his head frostily, grabbed a roll from the basket and took an aggressive bite. Several minutes passed when he finally broke his silence.

"I had an argument with Joseph today. He

comes here all the time, but when I ask if we can go to his house, he always makes excuses or changes the subject. He's borrowed loads of my games, but I haven't played with any of his."

Dad gently tapped his glass with his fork to grab Sulaiman's attention, as well as Hannah and Musa who were loudly squabbling over a carton of juice. Musa wanted to pour himself a drink, but Hannah noticed he was spilling it all over the table and was trying to help him. Dad tapped the glass again until the table went quiet. Everyone looked in Dad's direction.

"We should always give or share the best of what we have, whether it's our time and energy, or our money and toys. We should give wholeheartedly for the sake of Allah without expecting anything in return. Allah's reward is enough with 10 to 700 times

reward for every good deed."

"Do you remember when Mum gave my new coat to that little girl?" Hannah interrupted excitedly, recalling the time her school had a foreign exchange pupil who had not anticipated how cold it would be in England. "I was really sad 'cos I thought I wouldn't have a coat in the winter, but auntie gave me another one and it was even better than the coat mum gave away!"

"Exactly!" Dad emphasized. "Allah will never cause you to lose out when you give generously to those in need. In fact, Allah will increase you and give you something even better in return. Has Joseph told you about his family circumstances, Sulaiman?"

"What do you mean?" Sulaiman replied looking puzzled.

"A few months ago, a war broke out in Joseph's country. It got so bad that he and his family had to leave in just the clothes they were wearing. Everything they had was left behind. Since coming to this country, they've had to stay in a hostel," his dad explained.

"Well, I don't mind. I can still visit him in his hostel, can't I?" Sulaiman suggested naively.

"It's not that simple. Joseph is living with his parents, and his brother and sister in just *one* room. They also have to share a kitchen and bathroom with other families in the hostel. He might be embarrassed to invite you over because its overcrowded and maybe he hasn't got any games for you to play with anyway."

"But he said his dad's a doctor," Sulaiman interrupted. He knew doctors get paid well, as Ibrahim's dad was a GP and he was always coming into school with new stuff.

"His dad *is* a doctor, but he hasn't been

able to work in this country," Dad replied.

Sulaiman stared at his father looking a bit lost. He felt bad. Perhaps he didn't know Joseph as well as he thought he did. How could he have spent so much time with his best friend and not have known the situation he was in?

"I thought he didn't invite me to his house because he was ashamed of *me*, not because he was ashamed of where he lived," Sulaiman whispered with embarrassment. "And I thought he didn't let me play with his games because he didn't trust me, not because he didn't have any."

Sulaiman couldn't sleep very well that night. He felt guilty for having misjudged Joseph, and ashamed that he hadn't made any excuses for Joseph's behaviour. Although Sulaiman was far from being rich, he had never known what it was like to be really poor. He then remembered what his dad said over dinner about giving and sharing. He was determined to make it up to Joseph in some way.

Chapter 5

The next day at school Sulaiman eagerly searched for Joseph at breakfast club. Joseph was just finishing off the last mouthful of his toast.

"I've got something for you!" Sulaiman beamed excitedly handing him a bag full of toys and games he'd found lying around in his bedroom. "My dad told me why you don't have many toys, so I thought you could have some of mine."

Joseph peered inside the bag and scowled.

"What do you think I am – a charity case?" he snarled tossing the bag aside. It slid across the shiny table and crashed onto the floor. The bag split open and some of the toys broke on impact.

"What did you do that for?" Sulaiman remarked, looking hurt and shocked by Joseph's reaction. "I thought you'd be pleased."

"Well, I'm not. I don't need your rubbish!" Joseph huffed. "Before I came to this country, I had lots of games just like you. I wore really nice clothes. I had my own bedroom, in my own house. I had a garden and a bike...". Tears welled up in Joseph's eyes as he recalled fond memories of home.

Sulaiman looked at the broken toys

scattered across the floor. Joseph did have a point. They were a bit shabby. Then he remembered what his dad said around the dinner table.

I should have given him better ones than these. Sulaiman grimaced to himself. *If I don't want them, why would anyone else want them?*

Joseph continued ranting until he noticed Sulaiman was quiet.

"Why aren't you saying anything?" He asked defensively.

"I don't want to fight. I was only trying to help," replied Sulaiman calmly.

Joseph thought for a moment, "I'm sorry," he mumbled humbly. "I just didn't want you to pity me, that's all."

Sulaiman bit his lip and tried to think of a good response, because in truth, he *did* pity him, but he didn't want to hurt his feelings any more than he already had.

"Why would you think that?" Sulaiman asked feebly.

"Because you think I'm poor," Joseph replied rolling his eyes, "and I've got no toys or games."

"It's not a big deal," Sulaiman insisted placing his hand gently on Joseph's shoulder to reassure him.

"What do you mean? Of course, it's a big deal!" Joseph snapped shrugging Sulaiman's hand away. He picked up a toy from the floor and snapped it in half in frustration. "It's hard when you've got no money. I was never this poor back home."

Sulaiman stared at the broken toy Joseph was waving around in his hand. *I liked that toy.* He thought to himself almost regretting giving it to him. *It was a bit scratched but at least it still worked. I should have kept it.*

He then remembered what his dad said

about only focusing on Allah when giving things and not to expect anything in return. *I thought he would have thanked me, but Allah is al-Shakoor, the Most Grateful and He will reward me for my intention.* It was a tense moment and Sulaiman felt bad. He tried to think of more sayings about the blessings of being poor to comfort Joseph.

"Anyway, there's nothing wrong with being poor," Sulaiman remarked, trying to lift his mood. "It's a test but there's also rewards in it."

"Rewards for what?" Joseph asked looking confused and still a bit irritated. Sulaiman had never talked to him about Islam before. Joseph would wait for Sulaiman to pray at lunchtimes, but he never asked any questions, so they never really talked about religion.

"In Islam, Allah rewards poor people for being patient, as it's easy to complain, isn't it?" Joseph looked away sheepishly, realising he had spent the past few minutes moaning about his situation. Sulaiman grimaced realising he had been too blunt and tried to think of something else to say to save Joseph any further embarrassment. He quickly remembered his conversation with his dad.

"Poor people can earn rewards by giving in charity," he blurted.

"How can they give in charity when they haven't got any money?" Joseph responded angrily. "That doesn't make sense!"

"No, I don't mean money," Sulaiman replied swiftly, feeling his body heat rise and radiate through his jumper from the stress. "You can give in so many other ways..."

But it was too late. Joseph grabbed his backpack, barged past him and stormed out the room.

"Urghhhh! Why?" Sulaiman groaned

loudly in frustration. "Now I've got to pick up all this mess *and* fix the other one I've just made with Joseph."

* * *

The first lesson of the day was maths. As Sulaiman entered the classroom, he noticed Joseph wasn't sitting in his usual seat and he refused to give Sulaiman direct eye contact despite seeing him come in. Sulaiman reluctantly sat at his desk next to the empty seat. After several minutes the maths teacher arrived. He approached the front of the class and placed some papers on top of his desk.

"I'm going to test you all on the topics we've covered so far this term," he announced looking around the room. "Joseph! Why aren't you in your seat?"

Joseph glanced over at Sulaiman coldly

and folded his arms.

"I don't want to."

"But you're in Adam's seat, can you move back to where you usually sit so Adam can sit down, please."

Joseph remained in his seat; arms folded.

"Joseph, I'm not going to tell you again. You need to move back to your own seat," the teacher insisted. Joseph pursed his lips and still refused to move. Sensing the tension between Sulaiman and Joseph the maths teacher picked up the test papers from the desk and gave them to a boy sitting in the front row.

"Jack, hand these out to the class, please. I'm going to be out of the room for a few minutes, but you can all start as soon as you receive your test paper. Joseph and Sulaiman follow me, please."

Sulaiman and Joseph rose from their desks

making a loud scaping noise with their chairs across the floor. Joseph was nearer to the door and left first with Sulaiman following behind him.

"Have you two fallen out?" asked the teacher in the hallway. Both remained mute and stared away from each other. "You need to resolve whatever dispute you have so you can go back and sit at your desks."

There was a long uncomfortable silence. "Right, I'm going to leave you for five minutes to talk it out. I want to see it all resolved by the time I come back, otherwise I'm going to give you both an after-school detention."

"I'm not having a detention." Sulaiman insisted as soon as the teacher disappeared out of sight.

"I'm not either." Joseph tutted giving Sulaiman a mean stare.

"It was you who left your seat. Why should

I get a detention for something you did?" Sulaiman persisted. "I don't even know why you're so mad at me."

"You have no idea what it's like to be poor and you're telling me to stop complaining and just give money in charity," Joseph mocked sarcastically.

Sulaiman gasped wide-eyed.

"I never said it like that! You left before I could explain properly. I meant poor people are rewarded if they are patient 'cos their life's not as easy as rich people. And when I said poor people can earn rewards for giving in charity, I didn't mean by giving money. Charity can be given in other ways... like a smile is charity. So is cheering someone up or removing something harmful in the road. You help me with my maths homework, don't you? That's giving your time and sharing knowledge with me, isn't it? And you showed me how to do tricks with my remote-controlled car. That's sharing your skills and talents. So, there's many ways to earn rewards for giving in charity even if you don't have money."

Joseph's shoulders slowly relaxed. He stared intensely at his scuffed shoes but couldn't stay serious for long.

"I'd still prefer to have money though."

He gestured rubbing his thumb quickly over his fingers.

Sulaiman chuckled and nodded in agreement.

"Then you can give me some!"

"I will!" Joseph insisted. "Then you can buy me some better games!"

Sulaiman was glad they were still friends, and even more glad that he wasn't going to have a detention.

Chapter 6

Several months had passed and life was improving for Joseph. He was getting good grades at school and had won several awards in sports tournaments. However, things were about to change. Everyday Sulaiman and Joseph would meet outside his hostel and walk to school together. But Joseph hadn't shown up for a couple of days.

Sulaiman was concerned, so he decided to pay him a visit on his way home after lessons. Standing on the doorstep of the hostel he pressed the intercom. Joseph's father answered and gave Sulaiman access into the building. He passed through a dimly lit corridor and up a flight of stairs. Joseph was waiting for him in the doorway.

The room was tiny for a family of five. There was hardly any room to move with all their worldly belongings crammed between the beds and the wardrobes. Sulaiman wondered how Joseph studied and was able to complete his homework. He didn't even have a desk. Joseph pushed the clothes off his bed to let Sulaiman sit down. He offered Sulaiman a drink and grabbed some snacks from a nearby shelf. Sulaiman was moved by his generosity, particularly as he didn't have very much to offer.

"Why haven't you been at school, have you been sick?" Sulaiman asked as he sipped some of his drink.

"No," Joseph responded wearily. "We've been told we can't stay in this country anymore and we've got to go."

"Go! Go where?" Sulaiman exclaimed almost choking on his gulp.

"Back to our own country."

"But you can't leave!" Sulaiman cried rising to his feet. Some black bags were jammed between the beds preventing him from moving so he quickly sat back down again. Joseph sighed heavily. He had heard his parents discussing the situation over and over again, night after night as he lay in his bed.

"My dad says we could appeal against the decision, but our lawyer is really busy with other cases, and he doesn't take on appeals."

"Get another lawyer then," Sulaiman

interrupted.

"We've tried but they can't help either. We were told we could pay for a private lawyer, but Dad can't afford it as he's not allowed to work here." Joseph sighed heavily and shook his head.

Sulaiman was lost for words. He tried to make Joseph smile with a few jokes but was unsuccessful. He wasn't in the mood to laugh or joke.

That night while Sulaiman was eating dinner with his family, he told his dad about Joseph's dilemma.

"What can we do? He's my best friend," Sulaiman pleaded.

"I'll ask your uncle," his dad suggested sympathetically. "He might know some people who can help." He left the table to make a phone call and agreed to meet Sulaiman's uncle the next day.

Chapter 7

When dad returned home from work the following day, Sulaiman rushed to the front door to greet him.

"So, what did Uncle say, can he do anything?"

"Give me a chance to get in through the door!" his dad laughed, scooped Sulaiman up in a bear hug and carried him through to the kitchen.

"Switch the kettle on and make me a cuppa. I'll get out of my work clothes. Then I can tell you all about it."

Sulaiman was stirring the milk into the mug of tea when his dad came back into the room. He pulled out a chair and sat down at the kitchen table.

"A few of us have donated some money to cover the cost of hiring another lawyer for Joseph's family," his dad explained. "We're still a bit short, but we can raise some more money in other ways."

"I've got some money you can put towards it!" Sulaiman exclaimed excitedly. "I was saving up for a game, but I don't mind not having it." His dad beamed with pride and ruffled Sulaiman's hair to show how pleased he was for his son's material sacrifice. "And maybe I can do a few jobs around the house to earn some extra money?" he suggested eagerly.

"Good idea! But I'm not paying you to tidy your room. You should be doing that anyway!" Dad laughed heartily, wagging his finger. "I'll ask your auntie if she has any odd jobs that need doing and I'll ask around the community. I'm sure people will be willing to donate. As soon as the lawyer is paid for, we'll just have to wait patiently and pray for a good outcome."

* * *

That week during a lunch break at school, Sulaiman noticed Joseph was unusually quiet. Despite Sulaiman's jokes, he still couldn't make Joseph smile.

"Are you going to eat that?" he asked, pointing to Joseph's pasta. Joseph shook his head and pushed his plate to one side.

"I'm not hungry," he said, clutching his tummy with both hands. Sulaiman's eyes bulged with delight at the thought of a second helping.

"What's the matter?" Sulaiman asked, tucking into a large mouthful of food.

"I didn't sleep properly last night. I kept remembering when they pointed a gun at my dad and threatened to kill him. They can't send us back – it's not safe. There's nothing to go back to anyway. They destroyed our house."

Sulaiman dropped his fork onto his plate in horror. He suddenly lost his appetite too. All the time they had known each other, Joseph had never spoken of his experiences of the war. Sulaiman had no words of comfort and felt equally helpless. The decision was with the lawyers and the court judge. It was going to be a long, agonizing wait.

"So, what did you do over the weekend, anyway?" Joseph asked quickly changing the subject.

"It was a bit rubbish actually," Sulaiman responded rolling his eyes. "Mum took us to the park, but I had to look after Musa and push him on the swings and slides." Joseph watched in amusement as Sulaiman angrily stabbed at a pasta shell and squished a pea with his fork as he recalled the experience.

"I had to look after my little brother back home too. Mum would send us to the market at weekends to buy food. I hated it as I had to hold his hand, and he was always soooo slow." Sulaiman tutted knowingly as he understood the struggle.

"I really miss it though," Joseph lamented bowing his head. Tears welled up in his eyes and he glanced away to hide his emotions.

"I can't go out for food here as we haven't got much money, and we have to rely on foodbanks." There was a long awkward pause, but Joseph quickly regained his smile.

"My brother's so messy. He'd get food down his chin and on his clothes… and I'd get mad having to clean him up. But I'd do anything to do it all again."

Sulaiman remembered how horrible he was to Musa by not sharing his sweets, and teasing him and making him cry. And although it was boring to take Musa on the swings, he would hate it if he couldn't go to the park with his family. Perhaps it was worth sacrificing some of his valuable time to make Musa happy.

"Next time we go to the park, come with us," Sulaiman suggested eagerly. "You can bring your little brother and he can play on the slide with Musa, and we can kick a ball around

and play with my remote-controlled car."

Joseph beamed approvingly and grabbed his fork. His appetite suddenly returned. He playfully stabbed at a pasta shell and gobbled it up. Sulaiman sensed a challenge and raced to stab another pasta shell with his fork. Taking it in turns they finished the last remains of the dish.

"Oh no! That wasn't my pasta, was it?" Sulaiman gasped feeling guilty for having taken the last mouthful. He reached inside his bag and grabbed a banana and bottle of drink.

"Here, take these to make up for it." Although Sulaiman was thirsty, he knew the reward and increased blessings in sharing food and reached across the table to fill his cup from the water jug instead.

Chapter 8

A few months later Joseph and his family received the phone call they had been waiting for. They sat in silence in the room in their hostel and waited for Joseph's dad to return to give them the news. He sat down on the end of the bed and exhaled loudly, hanging his head. He looked exhausted. Tears began to well up in Joseph's eyes.

"What did he say Dad, do we have to go back?" he asked urgently. His dad covered his face and wept. Joseph was confused and quickly sprung to his feet. He had never seen his father cry like that before and was convinced tears meant bad news.

"I don't understand! Do we have to go back or not?" he demanded.

"No!" his father cried, grabbing Joseph's mother and swinging her off her feet. "They said we can stay!"

Joseph was so excited he grabbed his school bag and ran out of the room without even a goodbye. He couldn't wait to tell Sulaiman who was waiting outside the hostel for their usual walk to school together.

"We can stay! We can stay!" Joseph shouted excitedly as he shook Sulaiman's shoulders. Sulaiman jumped up and down enthusiastically and hugged Joseph tight.

* * *

"Who's going to help make food for the picnic?" Sulaiman asked his family at dinner that night.

"What picnic?" his mum asked curiously as she placed Sulaiman's plate of food in front of him. "Have we been invited to a picnic?"

"Yes, you're all invited!" Sulaiman smiled confidently. "Joseph and his family have been told they can stay, and I want to throw a picnic in the park this weekend to celebrate."

"Oh, that's brilliant news!" Dad roared jubilantly. "I'll invite your uncle and auntie and your cousins. I'm sure those who were involved would love to hear about this and join the picnic too."

"I'll cook some chicken drumsticks and make a salad," Mum suggested generously.

"I'll make some chocolate chip cookies like the ones I made for the Scout fund-raiser!" Hannah chimed excitedly. "I've still got the recipe."

"And I'll help you eat it all!" Musa giggled raising his knife and fork in the air enthusiastically. Sulaiman was so pleased that his family were kind enough to volunteer their time to help him make the occasion a special one.

That weekend in the park, Sulaiman and his family were arranging the picnic food on a huge cloth laid out on the grass. One by one his uncle, auntie, and cousins arrived with foldaway seats followed by members of the community bringing various food dishes, drinks and snacks. In the distance Sulaiman spotted Joseph and his family approaching carrying blankets to sit on. He ran to greet him.

"I brought my football and remote-controlled car!" Sulaiman cried eagerly.

"I've got balloons and blowing bubbles," Musa squealed loudly when he saw Joseph's little brother. He ran to give him a hug, spilling half the bubble solution down his trousers, but he was too excited to care.

After everyone had eaten and celebrated, the older cousins took the younger children to play on the swings and slides in the playground. Sulaiman and Joseph decided to stay back and kick the football around.

"Shall we play with my remote-controlled car now?" Sulaiman suggested after a while, taking it out of its box. "Dad made me a proper ramp for it, look." He ran a few feet away to set it up and then returned to give Joseph the controller. "You can go first," he insisted.

They performed stunts and tricks with it on the grass all afternoon until it was eventually time to go home. As Sulaiman was packing away the car, he remembered how stingy he had been giving Joseph all his old toys and games.

"You're a better driver than me, you keep it," he said warmly, handing Joseph the box.

"I don't know what to say…." Joseph whispered, feeling quite choked up and overwhelmed.

"You don't have to say anything, just teach me how to do that 360-degree spin," replied Sulaiman, chuckling heartily.

Comprehension Questions

1. Why were Hannah and Musa upset with Sulaiman the day before Eid?
2. What trick could Joseph do with the remote-controlled car?
3. Why did Sulaiman think his friendship with Joseph was one-sided, and what were they arguing about during break time?

4. How many rewards will Allah bless us with for doing a good deed?
5. Is charity only about giving money? Can you think of anything else that we are encouraged to give?
6. Why wasn't Joseph happy with the toys Sulaiman gave? What could Sulaiman have done instead?
7. Why hadn't Joseph been to school for a few days and how did Sulaiman try to help?
8. What news did Joseph and his family receive and how did Sulaiman want to celebrate?
9. State three ways in which Sulaiman gave the best of what he had (remember he didn't just give money).
10. What skills, talents and abilities do you have that you could give to others as ways of charity?

Evidence from the Qur'an and Sunnah

Say, [*O Prophet*], *"Surely* [*it is*] *my Lord* [*Who*] *gives abundant or limited provisions to whoever He wills of His servants. And whatever you spend in charity, He will compensate* [*you*] *for it. For He is the Best Provider."*

Surah Saba (34:39)

Allah's Messenger (ﷺ) said,

"If any one of you improve (follows strictly) his Islamic religion then his good deeds will be rewarded ten times to seven hundred times for each good deed and a bad deed will be recorded as it is."

Narrated by Abu Hurairah;
Sahih al-Bukhari.

The Messenger of Allah (ﷺ) said:

"Sadaqah does not decrease property; and Allah increases the honour of those who forgive; and no one will humble themself for Allah's sake except that Allah raises their status."

Narrated by Abu Hurairah;
Sahih Muslim.

The Messenger of Allah (ﷺ) said,

"Every joint of a person must perform a charity each day that the sun rises: to judge justly between two people is a charity. To help a man with his mount, lifting him onto it or hoisting up his belongings onto it, is a charity. And a good word is a charity. And every step that you take towards the prayer is a charity, and removing a harmful object from the road is a charity."

On the authority of Abu Hurairah; Sahih al-Bukhari & Sahih Muslim.

"A man said: 'O Messenger of Allah, which kind of charity is best?' He said: 'Giving charity when you are in good health, and feeling stingy, hoping for a long life and fearing poverty.'"

Narrated by Abu Hurairah; An-Nasa'i.

The Messenger of Allah (ﷺ), said,
"The food on one person is enough for two, the food of two is enough for four, and the food of four is enough for eight."

Narrated by Jabir; Sahih Muslim.

Ibn Abbas informed, *'I heard the Prophet (ﷺ) say, "He is not a believer whose stomach is filled while his neighbour goes hungry."'*

Al-Adab al-Mufrad.